JOHNNY LONGLEGS

HAPPY READING!

This book is especially for:

_____

Suzanne Tate,
Author—
brings fun and
facts to us in her
Nature Series.

James Melvin,
Illustrator—
brings joyous life
to Suzanne Tate's
characters.

Suzanne and James in costume

JOHNNY LONGLEGS
A Tale of Big Birds

Suzanne Tate

Illustrated by James Melvin

Nags Head Art

To Chris

who lives on
through her wonderful words

Library of Congress Control Number 2005928408
ISBN 978-1-878405-50-0
ISBN 1-878405-50-0
Published by
Nags Head Art, Inc., P.O. Box 2149, Manteo, NC 27954
Copyright© 2005 by Nags Head Art, Inc.

Johnny Longlegs was a big bird.
He was a young Great Blue Heron.

He had long legs and big toes.

Johnny and his parents lived in a wet
and soggy place called a marsh.

Great Blue Herons were the
biggest birds there.

Johnny's father, Big Cranky, was four feet tall,
and his wings were six feet across!
He was bigger than Johnny's mother,
Mama Longlegs.

The big herons looked for food both
day and night.
Their long legs helped them hunt.

They ate whatever they could catch
— fish, frogs, bugs and snakes.

Johnny's mother and father taught him
everything he knew.
"Now, if you tiptoe like this," Big Cranky said,
"you can catch a lot of fish."

Big Cranky slowly lifted one long leg
after the other.

"Oh, I know how to hunt," Johnny squawked.
"Watch me now. I'm ready to grab a fish."

But he splashed along in the marsh,
and all the little fish swam away.

"Kraak! You'll have to do better than that,"
squawked Big Cranky.
"Watch me carefully this time,
and you will learn how to hunt."

"Yes, your father is the best hunter
in the marsh," Mama Longlegs said.

Big Cranky stood as still as a statue.
His large toes helped him to stand
on one leg for a long time.

Suddenly, he stuck out his long neck
and grabbed a fish with his sharp beak!

"I can do that too," Johnny Longlegs thought.
He went to a place where no one could see him.
Then, Johnny tried to tiptoe.
And he tried to stand still.

Soon, he caught a little fish.
"Now I can hunt like a big bird!"
the young heron thought happily.

About that time, Johnny saw something dark in the water. "There's a fish," he thought.

He dived for it with his sharp beak.
But it was a squiggly, wiggly snake.
It turned its head and tried to bite Johnny!

But the young heron quickly threw the snake
onto the marsh.
The snake was stunned.

Then, Johnny picked it up
and gulped it down!

Johnny Longlegs felt like a big bird.
But suddenly, he was afraid!
He wasn't alone.

There was a strange pink bird
standing in the marsh.

Johnny Longlegs was excited!
"I've never seen a bird like that," he thought.

He quickly flew to the marsh where his parents were.
"Mama, Mama! I saw a strange, scary bird
— a pink one with long legs."

Mama Longlegs was standing quietly in the marsh.
She was cleaning herself with a powder
made from her own feathers.

"You must be mistaken," his mother said.
"We never see any pink birds in our marsh."

"But I saw it — I really did!" Johnny squawked.
Big Cranky was nearby and heard him.
"What are you squawking about?" he asked.

Johnny Longlegs told his father
about the strange big bird.

........Johnny squawked.

"You don't need to be afraid," Big Cranky said,
"just because it is a bird of a different feather."

"I will fly with you to see it," he said.
The two blue herons flew to the spot
where Johnny saw the strange bird.

There it was — a big bird with pink feathers
— standing alone in the marsh.

About that time, HELPFUL HUMANS came along.
Johnny and Big Cranky quickly
flew to the top of a tree.

They were skittish and didn't like
to be near HUMANS.

But the HELPFUL HUMANS were only there
to watch and count the birds.
They were surprised to see a pretty pink one.

"I have been reading a book in school about pink birds," a young girl said. "They are called flamingos. The shrimp they eat makes their feathers pink."

"This flamingo is far from its home and must be lost," her father said. "It will soon be too cold for it to stay here."

Johnny and Big Cranky flew back to the marsh
where Mama Longlegs was feeding.
They told her about the pink bird.

"We will leave that strange bird alone so it can
catch the food it needs," she said.
"There is plenty here for all of us."

But the flamingo flew away one day.
"That pink bird is smart like we are,"
Mama Longlegs said.
"It knows that cold weather is coming."

"We big birds always know
what is best for us to do."

Johnny Longlegs flew to the top of a tree.
"Kraack!" he squawked.
He felt proud to be a big bird!